This book is dedicated to my children,
Kaeden, A'Niyah, Malachi, and Amiri.
Thank you for being my inspiration for writing and
telling stories for the world to read.

To my fiancé, Anthony, thank you for
motivating me to get out of my comfort zone and
be fearless in pursuing my goals.

And to my family and friends, thank you
for all your encouraging words and
advice throughout this process.

I Love You All!

First Printing, July 2020

ISBN 978-0-578-71950-4

Kyle's Twinventure

created by
Demiko Picott

illustrated by
Hayley Moore

Kyle was an only child.

He loved spending
time with his
Mommy and Daddy,

but he also was lonely and dreamed
of having a sibling to play with.

So when his mommy and daddy told him he was going to have not one sibling,

but two twin brothers, he was so excited. He could hardly wait.

When the twins were in his mommy's belly,
he would lay next to her and talk to the babies
about all the things they would do together.

They would play
basketball, watch movies,

play tag, dance,

and eat
ice cream!

Then he sang all his favorite songs to his mommy's belly. Kyle wanted his baby brothers to know he was ready for them.

After months of
patiently waiting,
his brothers were born.
Their names were
Michael and Miles.

Kyle went to the hospital to visit them. His mommy and daddy let him hold the new babies, but he had to be very careful.

They were so small and they didn't
look like they were going to be able
to play ball anytime soon.
He realized that all the things he talked
about doing with the twins had to wait.

When his brothers came home from the hospital, Kyle quickly decided that having twin brothers was a lot of work.

He helped his mommy feed them, throw away diapers,

and watch them while they slept, which was a lot.

They were not fun at all.
He didn't mind because he loved his
baby brothers, but he sure wished
they'd start growing up fast.

As Michael and Miles got older, they started to crawl. Kyle got excited because he thought they would be able to play with him now.

It was just more work.
He had to help his mommy
and daddy stop them from
getting into everything.

Whenever he tried to play
a game with them, they crawled off
in two different directions.

He felt like they were playing their own
little game because they would smile
and laugh when he had to run after them.

This was not what he wanted to play.

The twins continued to grow and learn new things. They could finally walk and talk so Kyle was ready for all the fun activities he had planned.

Michael and Miles didn't want to do the same games as him though.

They enjoyed building things with blocks, playing with cars, and singing their ABC's and numbers.

Kyle felt even more
lonely because they
loved the same things and
had each other to play with all day.

Kyle came up with
a plan to trick them
into playing with him.

He took all the blocks,
cars, and sing-along
toys and hid them.

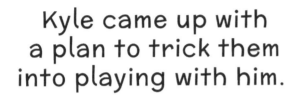

He was sure if they couldn't find their toys
that they would play with him.

"Let's play tag" he told them.
He tagged Michael and
started running,

but Michael
stood there
and cried.

Then he tagged Miles and ran away. Miles started to cry, too.

He was very disappointed.
His plan didn't work.
The twins stomped their feet and demanded their toys back.

So Kyle came up with another idea.
He tried to play basketball with Miles.
Miles did not want to play, and when
Michael came over with a toy car,

Miles ran off with his twin brother.

Kyle was disappointed again. He just couldn't get his baby brothers to have any fun with him.

It wasn't long before Kyle began to cry.

Michael and Miles looked at their
big brother, then looked at each other,
and walked over to him.

They gave him
a great big hug
and handed
him a car.

They grabbed his hand and all three of them sat on the floor playing cars on a tiny race track.

Kyle realized that maybe he needed to do
some of the activities that the twins enjoyed
doing right now. Eventually they may love
some of the things he loved.

Kyle and his brothers started
to play, laugh, dance, and
sing songs together.

He was
breaking up fights,
getting snacks,

and having to
be responsible for
them. But he was
having fun, too.

Kyle didn't know how hard it would
be being a big brother to twins,
but he loved them and they loved him.

And he wouldn't change it for anything.

CPSIA information can be obtained
at www.ICGtesting.com
Printed in the USA
LVHW071812100920
665517LV00016B/711

9 780578 719504